DATE DUE			
DE 18 91			
SE 20 '95			

BL

For
Catherine and Sarah

GO TELL IT TO THE TOUCAN
A Bantam Little Rooster Book/November 1990

PRINTING HISTORY
Published in Great Britain by Walker Books in 1990

Little Rooster is a trademark of Bantam Books, ·
a division of Bantam Doubleday Dell Publishing Group, Inc.

Library of Congress Cataloging-in-Publication Data
West, Colin.
Go tell it to the toucan / Colin West.
p. cm.
"A Bantam little rooster book"—T.p. verso.
Summary: Animals all over the jungle look for the toucan so he can tell
the animals to come to a party for elephant's birthday, and while
they search for that bird, they spread the word themselves.
ISBN 0-553-05889-4
[1. Jungle animals—Fiction. 2. Birthdays—Fiction.] I. Title.
PZ7.W51744Go 1990 89-18122
[E]—dc20   CIP
AC

Published simultaneously in the United States and Canada

Bantam Books are published by Bantam Books, a division of
Bantam Doubleday Dell Publishing Group, Inc. Its trademark, consisting of
the words "Bantam Books" and the portrayal of a rooster, is Registered in
U.S. Patent and Trademark Office and in other countires. Marca Registrada,
Bantam Books, 666 Fifth Avenue, New York, New York 10103.

Printed in Italy

0 9 8 7 6 5 4 3 2 1

Go tell it to the toucan

Written and illustrated by
Colin West

A BANTAM LITTLE ROOSTER BOOK
NEW YORK · TORONTO · LONDON · SYDNEY · AUCKLAND

"Hey, today it is my birthday!"
said the elephant one morning.
"I'll go tell it to the toucan.
Then he'll tell everybody,
and we can have a party—
a birthday jamboree!"

Old Jumbo looked around him,
but he couldn't find the toucan.
So instead he told the tiger:
"Today it is my birthday!
Please go tell it to the toucan.
Then he'll tell everybody,
and we can have a party—
a birthday jamboree!"

The tiger looked around him,
but he couldn't find the toucan.
So instead he told the warthog,
and the warthog told the hippo:

"Today is Jumbo's birthday!
Please go tell it to the toucan.
Then he'll tell everybody,
and we can have a party—
a birthday jamboree!"

The hippo looked around him,
but he couldn't find the toucan.
So instead he told the lion,
and the lion told the bullfrog,
and the bullfrog told the zebra:

"Today is Jumbo's birthday!
Please go tell it to the toucan.
Then he'll tell everybody,
and we can have a party—
a birthday jamboree!"

The zebra looked around him,
but he couldn't find the toucan.
So instead he told the rabbit,
and the rabbit told the rhino,
and the rhino told the lizard,
and the lizard told the panda:

"Today is Jumbo's birthday!
Please go tell it to the toucan.
Then he'll tell everybody,
and we can have a party—
a birthday jamboree!"

The panda looked around him,
but he couldn't find the toucan.
So instead he told the ostrich,
and the ostrich told the tortoise,
and the tortoise told the cricket,
and the cricket told the leopard,
and the leopard told the monkey:

"Today is Jumbo's birthday!
Please go tell it to the toucan.
Then he'll tell everybody,
and we can have a party—
a birthday jamboree!"

The monkey looked around him,
and upon the highest treetop
at long last he found the toucan!
So the monkey told the toucan
what Old Jumbo told the tiger,
what the tiger told the warthog,
what the warthog told the hippo,
what the hippo told the lion,
what the lion told the bullfrog,
what the bullfrog told the zebra,
what the zebra told the rabbit,
what the rabbit told the rhino,
what the rhino told the lizard,
what the lizard told the panda,
what the panda told the ostrich,
what the ostrich told the tortoise,
what the tortoise told the cricket,
what the cricket told the leopard,
what the leopard had just told him:

"Today is Jumbo's birthday!
Go tell everybody please,
and then we'll have a party—
a birthday jamboree!"

So the toucan looked around him.

He looked behind the bushes...

and he looked among the flowers...

and he looked down by the river....

The toucan looked all over,
but he still could find nobody.
So he went to tell Old Jumbo
there could be no jamboree....

But when the toucan found him,
Old Jumbo cried, "Hello!
Thanks for telling everybody
all about my birthday...."

"You're a really clever toucan.
Now come and join my party—